W9-CFB-319

Colorful Cars

Patricia Harris

illustrated by
Harold Poncelet

PowerKiDS
press

NEW YORK

Published in 2018 by The Rosen Publishing Group, Inc.
29 East 21st Street, New York, NY 10010

First Edition

Managing Editor: Nathalie Beullens-Maoui
Editor: Elizabeth Krajnik
Book Design: Michael Flynn
Interior Layout: Rachel Rising
Illustrator: Harold Poncelet

Cataloging-in-Publication Data

Names: Harris, Patricia.
Title: Race Cars Can Go / Patricia Harris.
Description: New York : PowerKids Press, 2018. | Series: Colorful cars | Includes index.
Identifiers: ISBN 9781538320914 (pbk.) | ISBN 9781538320938 (library bound) | ISBN 9781538320921 (6 pack)
Subjects: LCSH: Colors–Juvenile fiction. | Automobile racing–Juvenile fiction.
Classification: LCC PZ7.1.H36 Rac 2018 | DDC [F]–dc23

Manufactured in the United States of America

CPSIA Compliance Information: Batch #BS17PK: For Further Information contact Rosen Publishing, New York, New York at 1-800-237-9932

Please visit: www.rosenpublishing.com and www.habausa.com

CONTENTS

At Mr. Fred's racetrack, six cars lived in a big garage. The red car belonged to Tansy. The yellow car belonged to Billy. The white car belonged to Max.

The blue car belonged to Alexa. And the purple car belonged to Mary Ann. But at night, the drivers were not around. The cars sat in the garage all alone.

The race cars did not sit quietly in the garage all night. Just after the night got very dark and the stars came out, the six cars began to talk.

The white car said, "Max turns my steering wheel too hard on the curves."

The red car said, "Tansy is always having to repair me during the races."

All the cars had things to say about their drivers. Then the yellow car said, "We should take ourselves for a drive on the racetrack. We can race better than our drivers."

So they all started their engines and drove slowly over to the starting line.

9

At the starting line, the purple car said, "Get ready. Start your engines. Spin your tires. And GO!"

The cars took off. Right away, the red car had to stop for repairs. But no one was around to do the work. Then the white car turned his steering wheel too hard and went off the track. Soon all the cars had problems.

The six cars all had to limp back to the garage. For the rest of the night, they helped each other fix the problems.

The next night, they all went out to the track again. They ran many races. Everyone won at least one time. They had fixed their problems. The blue car said, "Now we are really race cars!"

For many nights, the six cars went racing. Then one night, the purple car said, "I wonder what is outside the track fence? Have any of you been outside the fence?"

"No," said all the others. Right then they all decided to go see what was outside the fence. They started their engines and went out of the gate.

The cars saw many things they had never seen before. They saw tall trees with green leaves. They saw a small stream with many rocks.

Then the race cars passed a farm. They saw a big red barn and a white horse. They also saw a green tractor. The tractor was much bigger than they were.

They went even further until they came to a town. Here they saw even more new things. They saw a house with a fence around it, and a store with a bright light out front.

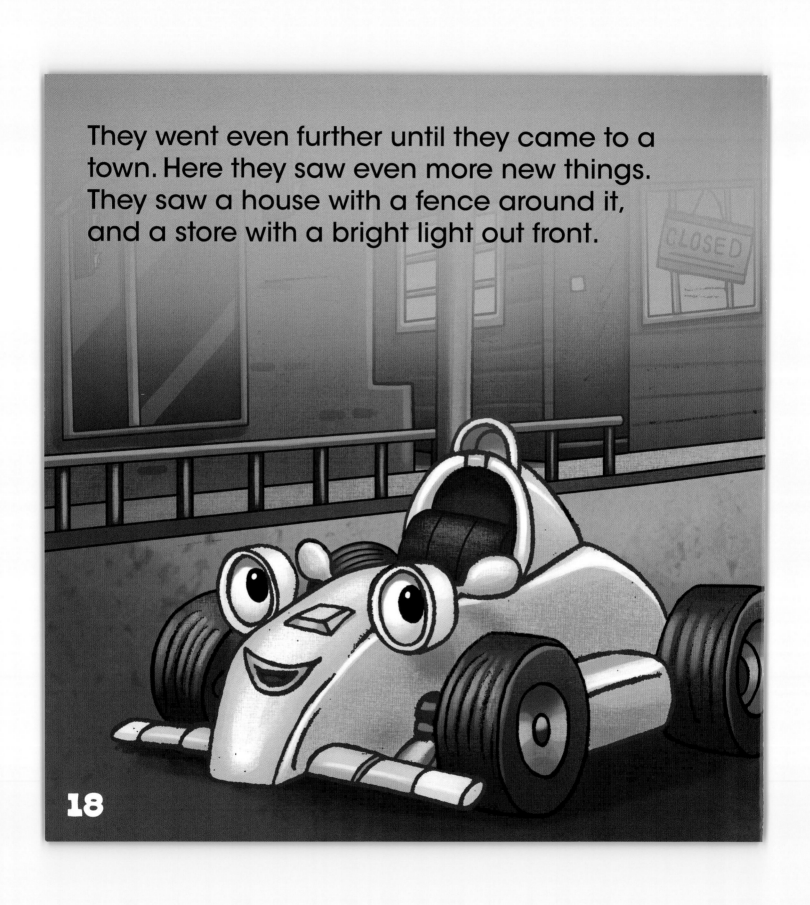

They saw a traffic light that went from red to yellow to green. They already knew about traffic lights because Mr. Fred's racetrack had one.

About the time the light turned green, the six cars saw that the night was turning into morning. They needed to go back to the track before the sun came up.

They quickly turned around and raced out of town. They went past all the things they had seen. They went faster, and faster, and faster.

They got into the garage just as the sun was coming up.

The next morning was Saturday and all the drivers came to race their cars. The cars were sitting in the garage all lined up and ready to go.

When the drivers finished the race, Max said, "My car did not go very fast today. Maybe I need to work on it." All the other drivers agreed. The six cars all yawned.

WORDS TO KNOW

fence

garage

tractor

INDEX